Taxation

Nicolas Brasch

Australia • Brazil • Japan • Korea • Mexico • Singapore • Spain • United Kingdom • United States

Taxation

Fast Forward
Turquoise Level 18

Text: Nicolas Brasch
Illustrations: Boris Silvestri
Editor: Cameron Macintosh
Design: Stella Vassiliou
Series design: James Lowe
Production controller: Seona Galbally
Photo research: Gillian Cardinal
Audio recordings: Juliet Hill, Picture Start
Spoken by: Matthew King and Abbe Holmes

Acknowledgements
The author and publisher would like to acknowledge permission to reproduce material from the following sources: Photographs by AAP Image/Ardiles Rante, p 9 bottom; Alamy/Tony Rusecki, cover right, pp 1 right, 18; Fairfax Photos/Jason South, 7 top/ Neil Newitt, p 20/ Paul Harris, p 6 top/ Wayne Taylor, p 7 bottom/ Dallas Kiponen, p 9 top/ Marco Del Grande, p 8/ Robert Pearce, p 12 bottom; Getty Images, p 11/ Alan Thornton, p 10/ Benelux Press, p 21/ Spencer Rowell, cover left, pp 1 left, 17; Newspix/Noel Kessel, p 22; Photolibrary/David Messent, p 12 top/ David R Frazier, p 13/ Kent Wood, p 6 bottom/ Lee Powers, p 15.

ISBN 978 0 17 012642 7
ISBN 978 0 17 012633 5 (set)

Cengage Learning Australia
Level 7, 80 Dorcas Street
South Melbourne, Victoria Australia 3205
Phone: 1300 790 853

Cengage Learning New Zealand
Unit 4B Rosedale Office Park
331 Rosedale Road, Albany, North Shore NZ 0632
Phone: 0800 449 725

For learning solutions, visit **cengage.com.au**

Printed in Australia by Ligare Pty Ltd
8 9 10 11 12 13 14 19 18 17 16 15

THE UNIVERSITY OF MELBOURNE

Evaluated in independent research by staff from the Department of Language, Literacy and Arts Education at the University of Melbourne.

Taxation

Nicolas Brasch

Contents

Chapter 1

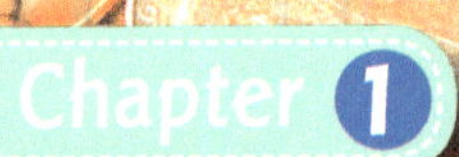

PAYMENTS TO THE GOVERNMENT

Taxation is the system that governments use to collect payments from a person, company or organisation.

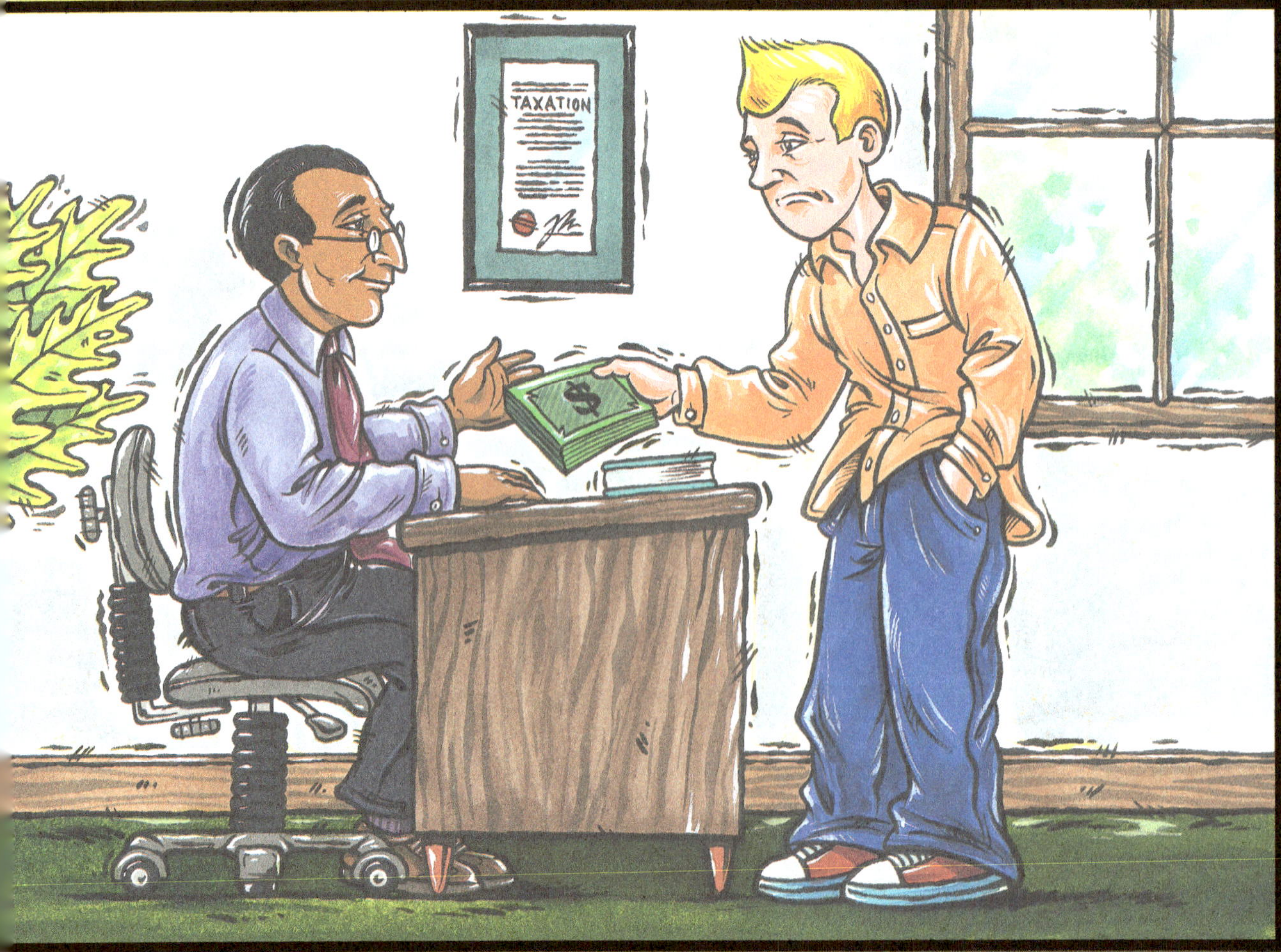

The payment of taxes is **compulsory**.
This means that a person, company or organisation has to pay tax, whether or not they want to.

Chapter 2

WHY GOVERNMENTS LEVY TAXES

Governments **levy** taxes on their citizens, and on companies and organisations, so that they will have money to spend.

Governments need to have money to spend because they are responsible for important areas of their citizens' lives.

Some of these important areas include:

- education

- defence

- emergency services

- transport.

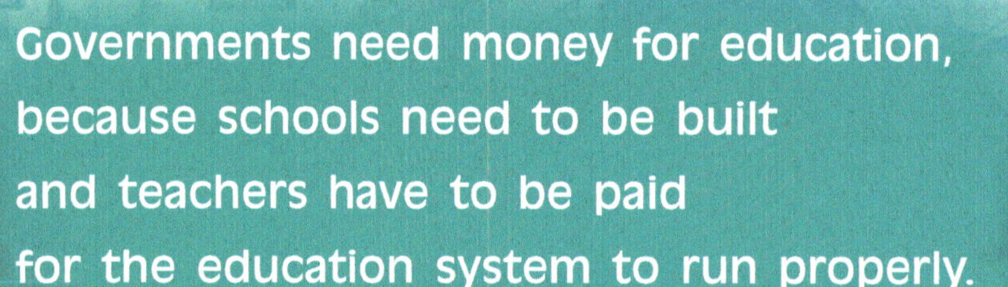

Governments need money for education, because schools need to be built and teachers have to be paid for the education system to run properly.

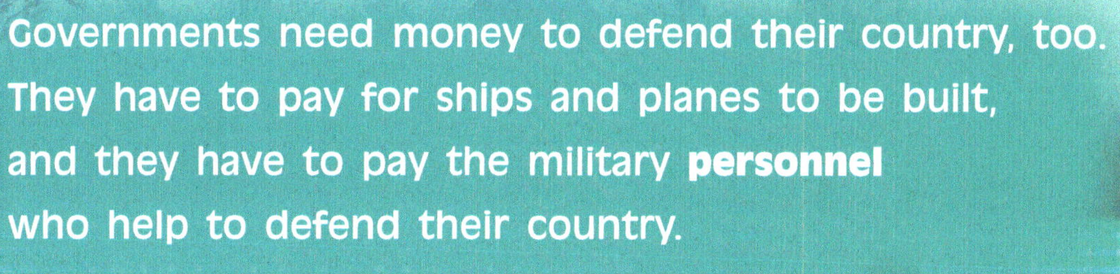

Governments need money to defend their country, too. They have to pay for ships and planes to be built, and they have to pay the military **personnel** who help to defend their country.

Governments also need money to help their citizens who get into trouble in other countries.

Governments also need money to pay for emergency services, like ambulance services, police and fire-fighting services.

They need to buy emergency service equipment, like ambulances, police cars, hoses, ladders and fire trucks. They must also pay emergency service personnel to do their jobs, and pay for them to be trained.

Governments also need money to run
the public transport system and the road network.
Trains, buses, ferries and trams have to be bought,
and drivers must be trained and paid
if the public transport system is going to work properly.

Old roads have to be repaired and new roads built if a road network is going to carry all the traffic that wants to use it.

So, governments need a lot of money to do their job. The way they get money is by taxing their citizens, companies and organisations.

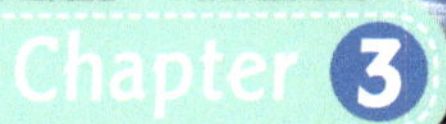

DIRECT TAXES

There are two main types of taxes.
These are direct taxes and indirect taxes.

Direct taxes are taxes that are paid directly from a person, company or organisation to a government.

The most common type of direct tax is **income** tax. Income tax is a tax on the amount of money people earn when they work.

The more money people earn, the more tax they have to pay.

Another type of direct tax is company tax.
Company tax is like income tax,
but it is a tax on the amount of money
a company earns in a year,
rather than the amount of money a person earns in a year.

Like income tax, the more a company earns, the more tax it has to pay.

Chapter 4

INDIRECT TAXES

Indirect taxes are an extra cost that governments put onto a good or service. Without this extra cost, the good or service would be cheaper.

Everybody pays the same amount of tax
on a good or service,
no matter how rich or how poor they are.

A goods and services tax is a type of indirect tax.
It is also called a sales tax.
A goods and services tax or sales tax
is an amount of money added to the price
of a good or service.

This extra amount is paid to the seller along with the rest of the money. But the seller has to pass this extra amount on to the government.

For example, a new computer may cost $500 without a tax on it.
But if a government has a tax on computers, the buyer has to pay $500 plus the tax.

So, if the computer costs $550 with the tax, the seller then has to give the extra $50 to the government.

Glossary

compulsory something that everybody has to do

government a group of people who rule a country

income the money a person earns from work

levy impose a fee

personnel the people who work for a particular organisation

Index